D1332269

A tale of moomunvalley

PUFFIN BOOKS

UK | USA | Canada | Ireland | Australia | India | New Zealand | South Africa

Puffin Books is part of the Penguin Random House group of companies
whose addresses can be found at global.penguinrandomhouse.com.

www.penguin.co.uk   www.puffin.co.uk   www.ladybird.co.uk

Penguin
Random House
UK

First published 2020
001

Characters and artwork are the original creation of Tove Jansson
Written by Richard Dungworth
Text and illustrations copyright © Moomin Characters™, 2020
All rights reserved

Printed in Italy
A CIP catalogue record for this book is available from the British Library

PB: 978-0-241-43225-9

All correspondence to:
Puffin Books, Penguin Random House Children's
80 Strand, London WC2R 0RL

FSC
www.fsc.org

MIX
Paper from
responsible sources
FSC® C018179

MOOMIN

and the

Spring Surprise

BASED ON THE ORIGINAL STORIES BY

Tove Jansson

PUFFIN

𝒜ll was still in 𝓜oominvalley, laying quietly in winter's frosty grip. The Moomin family, snug inside their stove-warmed house, were also laying quietly in their Long Winter Sleep. They were waiting for the sound of Too-Ticky's barrel-organ to rouse them, as it did every spring.

It was a different sound, however,
which woke Moomintroll.
  Ratta-tattle!
There it was again.

"Mamma! Pappa! Wake up!" whispered Moomin. But Moominmamma and Moominpappa slept soundly on – one dreaming of rose gardens, the other of daring exploits at sea.

"There's nothing for it," thought Moomin, trying his hardest to be brave. "I shall have to investigate that noise myself."

Moomin soon discovered what it was. The front door of the Moominhouse stood ajar, *ratta-tattle*-ing against its latch.

In the half-light outside, Moomin could see footprints in the snow. They were so small, he was sure he knew who had made them.

"Little My? What's *she* doing out of bed and up and about in winter?"

There was only one way to find out.

The footprint trail led into the forest – but not the forest as Moomin knew it. This icy world was strange and unsettling.

"What if spring isn't coming at all!?" worried Moomin. It was spring that brought his best friend Snufkin home to Moominvalley after his winter travels.

Moomin concentrated on his search for Little My to clear his mind of such an unhappy thought.

He looked for her under bushes, where she liked to play with her pet spider. She wasn't there.

He tried searching by the river where she liked to go tadpole hunting in spring. She wasn't there.

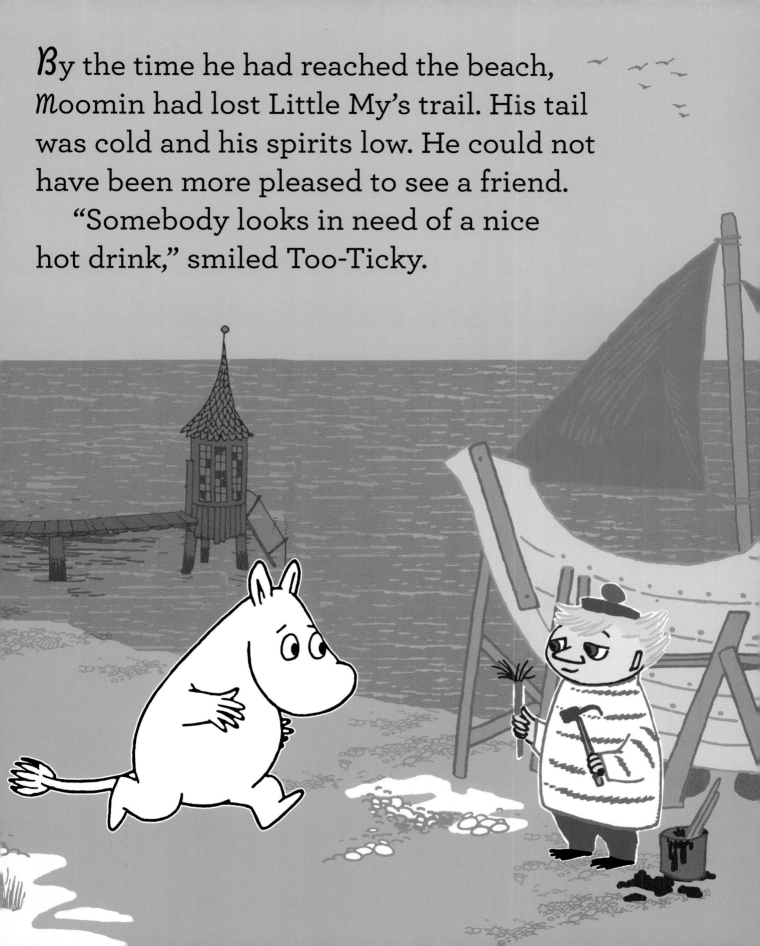

By the time he had reached the beach, Moomin had lost Little My's trail. His tail was cold and his spirits low. He could not have been more pleased to see a friend.

"Somebody looks in need of a nice hot drink," smiled Too-Ticky.

$\mathcal{I}$nside Too-Ticky's cosy winter home, $\mathcal{M}$oomin sipped warm cocoa and shared his fear that spring might not be coming.

"Are you *sure* you haven't seen any signs of spring?" asked Too-Ticky with a smile.

Moomin set out once more. As he continued his search a small orange creature crossed his path. "Looking for someone?" it enquired. "I can show you the best look-out place, if you like?"

Moomin followed the scampering squirrel – and soon found himself tackling the most daring, tummy-turning climb of his life. Up and up they clambered . . .

. . . to the very top of Moominvalley's highest waterfall.

"You can see the whole world from up here!" gasped Moomin.

But try as he might, he could spy no sign of Little My.

Then, as Moomin watched, the morning sun rose. As its rays warmed his nose and tail, his heart lifted. Was spring on its way after all?

Moomin's ears pricked as the faint sound of music rose from the valley below.

"That's Too-Ticky's barrel-organ! Spring!" exclaimed Moomin.

Suddenly bursting to see his family, Moomin headed for home as fast as his short legs would carry him.

In the first spring sunlight, the forest was changing. Plants were beginning to bud and blossom. Birds sang. The crisp air, full of the fresh green scents of new life, made Moomintroll's snout tingle.

As he reached the forest clearing he saw a tell-tale flash of red. "Little My!" he called out. "I've been looking *everywhere* for you!"

"*W*hy did you get up so early?" asked Moomin.
    "If you *must* know, mister busy-body," scowled Little My, "I wanted to catch an Ant Lion while it was still drowsy from its winter sleep. But I need a bigger jam jar."

"*There* you both are!" said a relieved Moominmamma. "Two empty beds gave me quite a surprise. Now, come along. You know the importance of a proper Spring Breakfast." She smiled at Moomin. "And we have a guest."

"Snufkin!" cried Moomin. "You're back!"
"You know me," grinned Snufkin.
"As reliable as the seasons."

The return of Moomin's best friend turned the family's Spring Breakfast into a fully fledged party. Moominmamma's homemade jam-topped pancakes had never tasted better.

That afternoon, Moomin made the daring climb
to the waterfall top again – this time with Snufkin,
with whom he shared *all* his favourite places.
As they sat side by side, Moomin thought
happily of the pond-dipping, den-building,
boat-sailing days that lay ahead...

. . . and decided that springtime, when
new adventures could begin, was
without doubt the best time of all.

The End